This book is dedicated to my mother and my father, who encouraged me to pursue my love of writing and to share it with others.

www.mascotbooks.com

Henry the Manatee

For more information, please contact:
Mascot Books
560 Herndon Parkway #120
Herndon, VA 20170
info@mascotbooks.com

Second Printing

Library of Congress Control Number: 2016910905

CPSIA Code: PRT0717B
ISBN: 978-1-63177-913-8

Printed in the United States

Henry
—the—
Manatee

Claire Lawrence

illustrated by Randi Zwicker

In a place called Hickory Bay,
Where the sun shines every day,

Lives a pear-shaped little manatee,
Who goes by the name of Henry.

Weighing a whopping two hundred pounds,

Making squeaky manatee sounds,

Henry floats along

To the beat of his own little song.

Henry's family tree
Didn't always live in the sea.

Hyrax

Henry

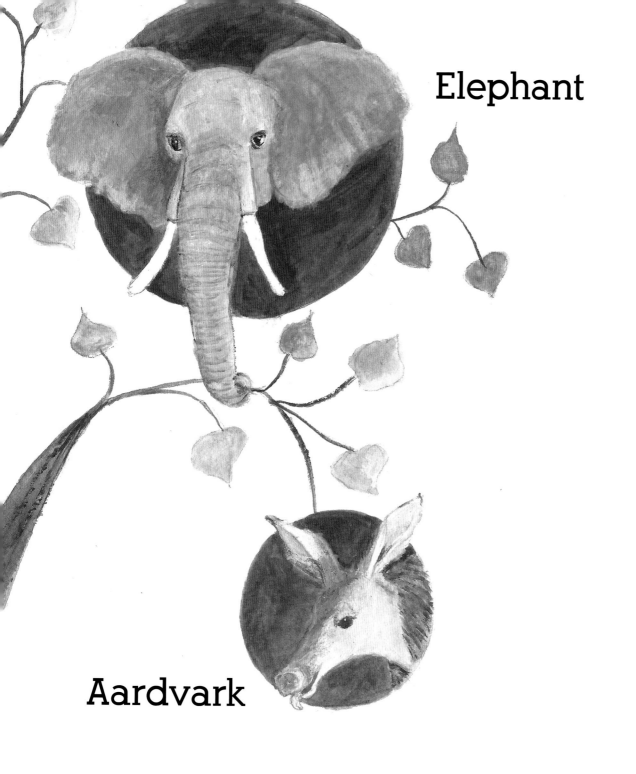

Elephant

Aardvark

He is related to elephants who walk on land
With four strong legs that can help them stand.

He's hairless, gray, and breathes air like you and me,
Dipping up, dipping down around the mangrove tree.

Learning from his mother, Henry will grow and thrive,
For the next two years, she will help him survive.

"Be back before dark, have fun but be safe,
Stay close to home and away from the wake…

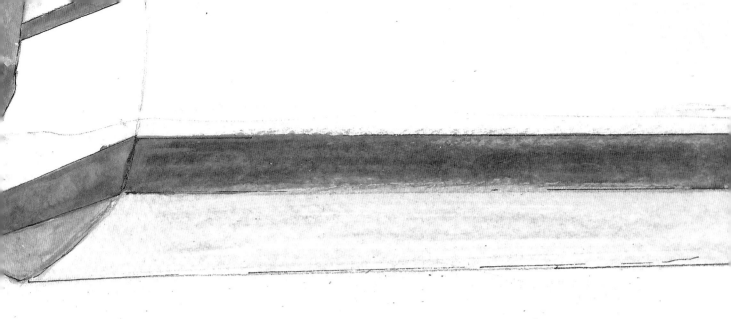

For that is what boats make with propellers that hurt,
Go more towards the bottom and always stay alert!"

He is gentle and kind,
You have nothing to fear,

And, if you get lucky,
He might just swim near.

Oh what a life out in the bay,
Nibbling seaweed, plants, and water flowers all day.

All the creatures he will meet and see,
There is so much to learn when you are a little manatee.

Manatees love the warmth
When the sun shines so bright,

The weather is great
And the water, just right!

But when the water sends chills up their spines,
They swim toward warm rivers and
leave the coolness behind.

There will come a day when he'll go off on his own
To create a new life and make a new home.

He will always love his mother,
Maybe shed a few tears,

But his life's just begun,
He has at least fifty more years.

He will swim and swim,
Up and down the streams,

In hopes of one day
Finding the manatee of his dreams.

And when he does,
It will be a glorious day,

But he'll never forget
Good ol' Hickory Bay!

Did You Know...

- A manatee is sometimes called a "sea cow."

- A baby manatee is a "calf."

- A female manatee must be at least five years old before she can give birth.

- A female can reproduce every two to five years.

- At birth, a manatee calf is three to four feet long and may weigh up to sixty-five pounds.

- A manatee has two flippers with three to four nails on each flipper.

- A manatee has a wrinkled face with a snout filled with whiskers.

- The average adult manatee is ten feet long and weighs between eight hundred to twelve hundred pounds.

- A manatee is a plant eater.

- A manatee can stay under water for up to twenty minutes by closing its nostrils.

- Half a manatee's day is spent sleeping in the water, surfacing every twenty minutes for air. The rest of the day, the manatee grazes in shallow waters that are three to six feet deep.

- A manatee usually swims about as fast as an adult human walks but can go much faster in short bursts.

- A manatee cannot survive in water that is colder than sixty degrees Fahrenheit.

About the Author

Claire Lawrence continues to work as a life skills and academic coach for children with social and behavioral challenges. Her love of animals has resulted in her writing delightful and whimsical nature stories. She lives in Bonita Springs, Florida with her husband, Tom, and two English labs.

About the Illustrator

Randi Zwicker has taught reading and language arts at both the elementary and middle school levels. Through her years of experience, she has realized the profound impact that illustrations can have when a young child is choosing a book to read. She has been drawing and painting since childhood and works with a variety of media. She lives in Bonita Springs, Florida with her husband, Bill, and cockatiel, Snow.

Have a book idea?
Contact us at:

info@mascotbooks.com | www.mascotbooks.com